ARMORED ADVENTURES

THE CRIMSON DYNAMO RETURNS!

P9-DGR-502

Adapted by D. R. Shealy
Based on the episode
"Iron Man vs. the Crimson Dynamo,"
by Brandon Auman
Illustrated by Patrick Spaziante

Random House 🏠 New York

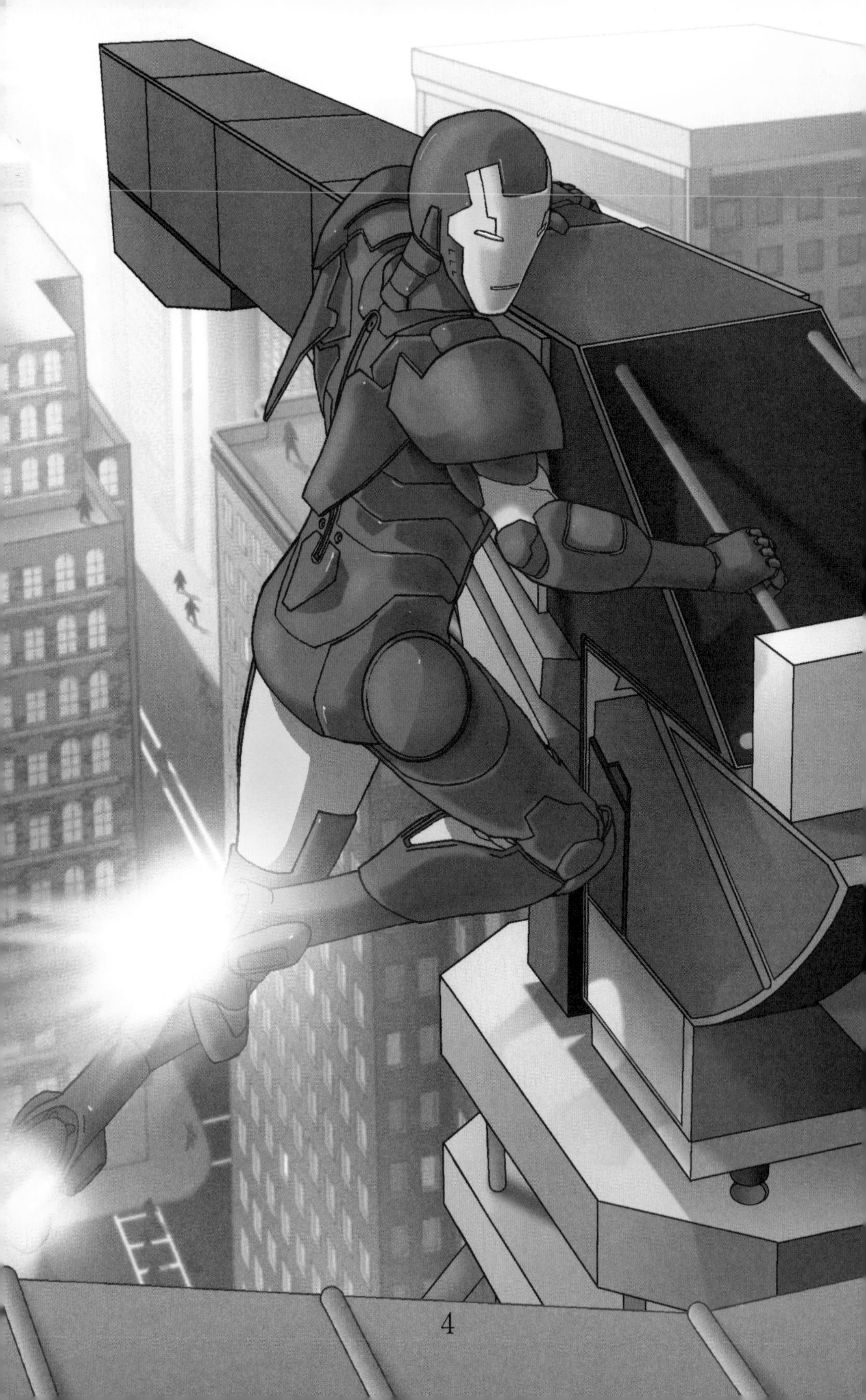

Dear Parent:

Congratulations! Your child is taking the first steps on an exciting journey. The destination? Independent reading!

STEP INTO READING® will help your child get there. The program offers five steps to reading success. Each step includes fun stories and colorful art. There are also Step into Reading Sticker Books, Step into Reading Math Readers, Step into Reading Write-In Readers, Step into Reading Phonics Readers, and Step into Reading Phonics First Steps! Boxed Sets—a complete literacy program with something for every child.

Learning to Read, Step by Step!

Ready to Read Preschool–Kindergarten
• big type and easy words • rhyme and rhythm • picture clues
For children who know the alphabet and are eager to begin reading.

Reading with Help Preschool–Grade 1
• basic vocabulary • short sentences • simple stories
For children who recognize familiar words and sound out new words with help.

Reading on Your Own Grades 1–3
• engaging characters • easy-to-follow plots • popular topics
For children who are ready to read on their own.

Reading Paragraphs Grades 2–3
• challenging vocabulary • short paragraphs • exciting stories
For newly independent readers who read simple sentences with confidence.

Ready for Chapters Grades 2–4
• chapters • longer paragraphs • full-color art
For children who want to take the plunge into chapter books but still like colorful pictures.

STEP INTO READING® is designed to give every child a successful reading experience. The grade levels are only guides. Children can progress through the steps at their own speed, developing confidence in their reading, no matter what their grade.

Remember, a lifetime love of reading starts with a single step!

For my mom,
who took me to the comic shop
—D.R.S.

For my wife and daughter, who make
me feel like a superhero every day
—P.S.

Visit us on the Web!
www.stepintoreading.com
www.randomhouse.com/kids
www.marvel.com

Educators and librarians, for a variety of teaching tools, visit us at
www.randomhouse.com/teachers

Library of Congress Cataloging-in-Publication Data
Shealy, Dennis R.
The crimson dynamo returns! / adapted by D. R. Shealy.
p. cm. — (Step into reading. Step 3)
"Based on the episode 'Iron Man vs. the Crimson Dynamo' by Brandon Auman."
ISBN 978-0-375-86178-9 (trade) — ISBN 978-0-375-96178-6 (library edition)
I. Iron Man (Television program). II. Title.
PZ7.S53767Cr 2009
[E]—dc22
2009005110

Printed in the United States of America
10 9 8 7 6 5 4 3 2 1

"Whoo-hoo!"
People cheered.
Iron Man had stopped
a falling crane.
He pushed it back into place
with his powerful armor.

Iron Man had a secret.
Only two people knew
that he was a boy
named Tony Stark . . .

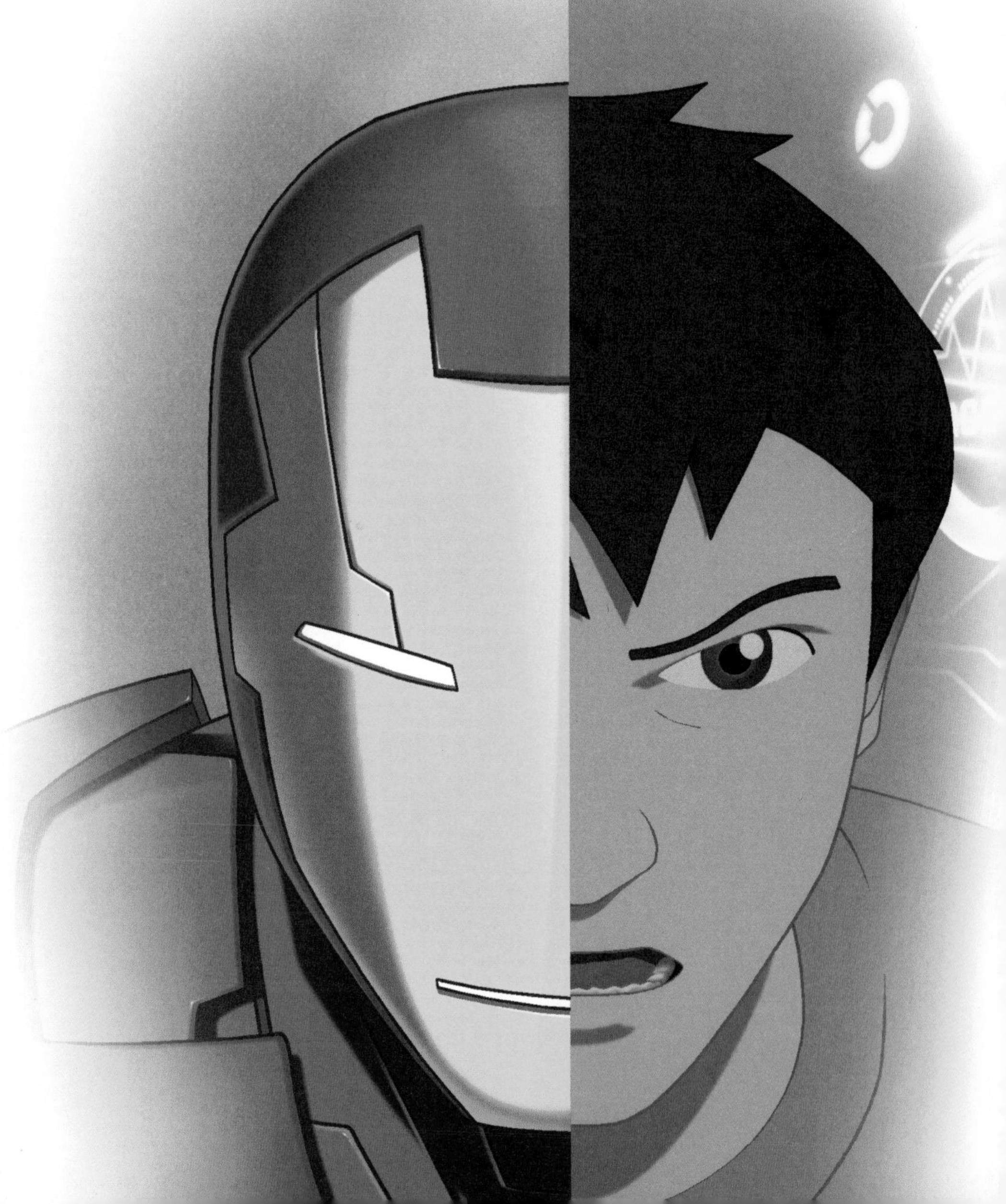

. . . Pepper Potts and
James "Rhodey" Rhodes.
And they were mad.
Tony was supposed
to help them
do a science project!

"I'm a little busy right now,"
said Iron Man over his comm link.
"*Whoa!*"

A flaming meteor
came shooting out of the sky!
It almost hit Iron Man!

BOOM!

The meteor smashed
into the ground!

Something moved inside the crater.

It was a man

in huge white armor!

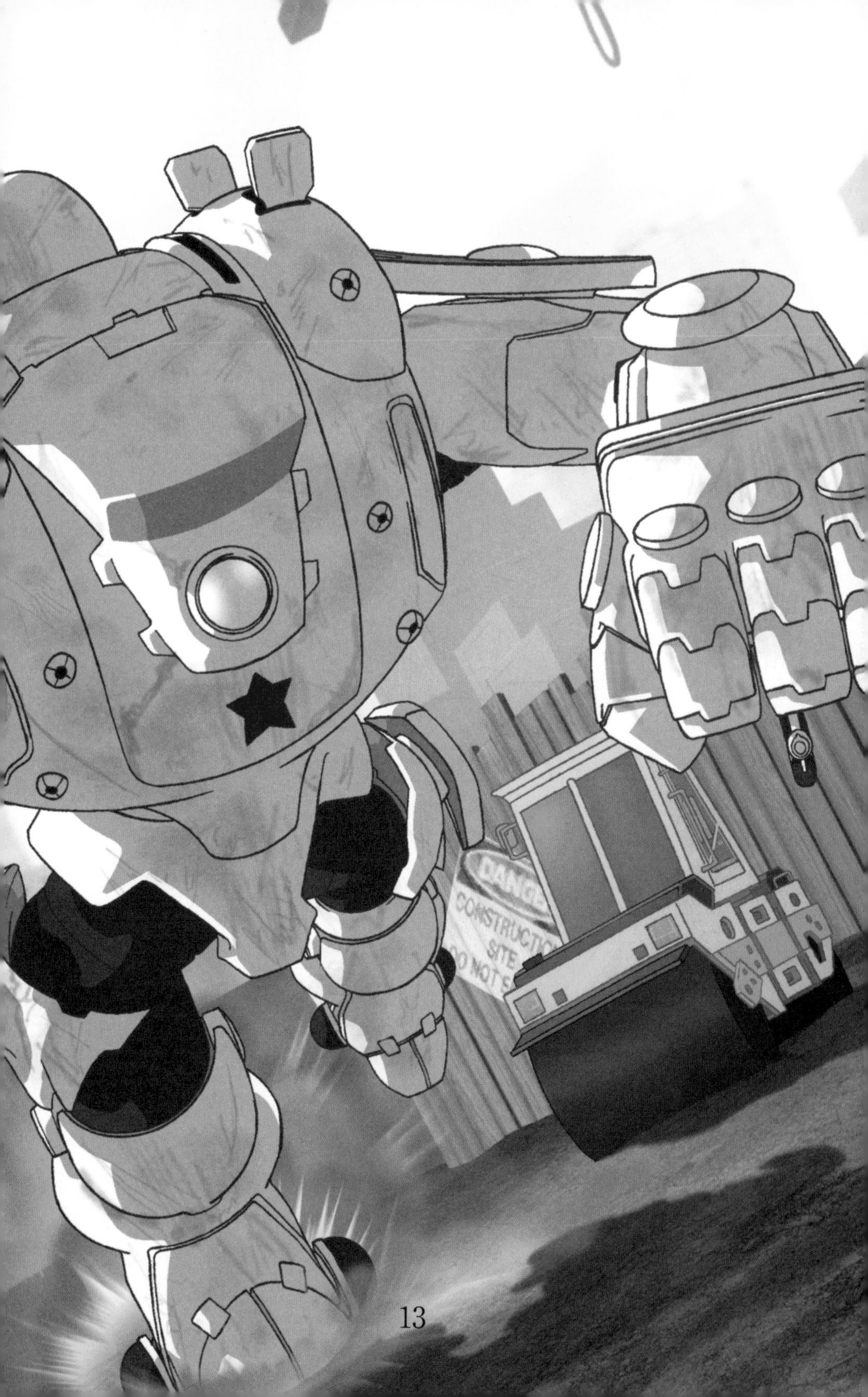
DANGE
CONSTRUCTIO
SITE
DO NOT S

"I'm going to be a little late getting back to the lab," Iron Man said.

Pepper gasped.

"That's the Crimson Dynamo

space suit," Rhodey said.

Suddenly,
the Crimson Dynamo
hurled a steamroller
right at Iron Man!

Iron Man caught
the steamroller
and set it down.

Iron Man slammed
into the Crimson Dynamo
and bounced right off!
The Crimson Dynamo
could not be stopped.

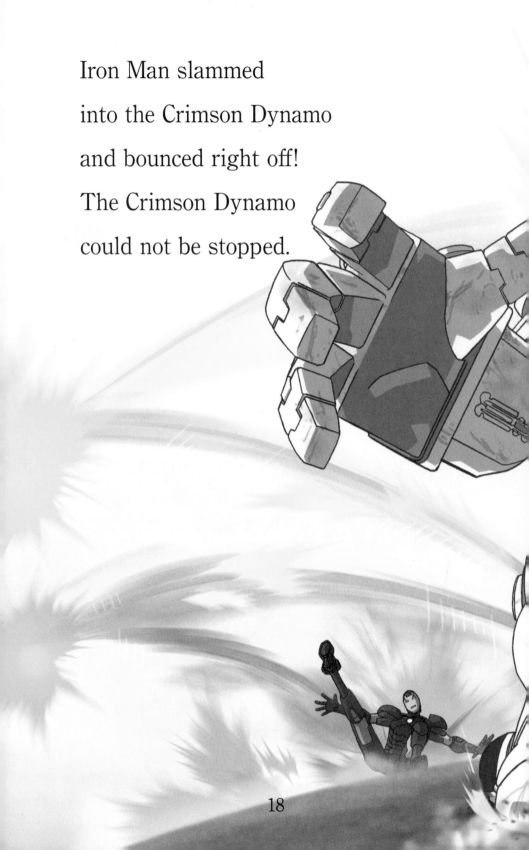

Iron Man tumbled to the ground.

"Tony!"

Pepper cried.

"Are you okay?"

"That armor is tough,"

Iron Man replied.

"I just got crushed!"

Then Iron Man spotted something.

It was a winged horse

painted on the armor.

"Look up this logo,"

Iron Man told Pepper.

She found it on her computer.

It was the logo
for a space lab
called Project Pegasus.

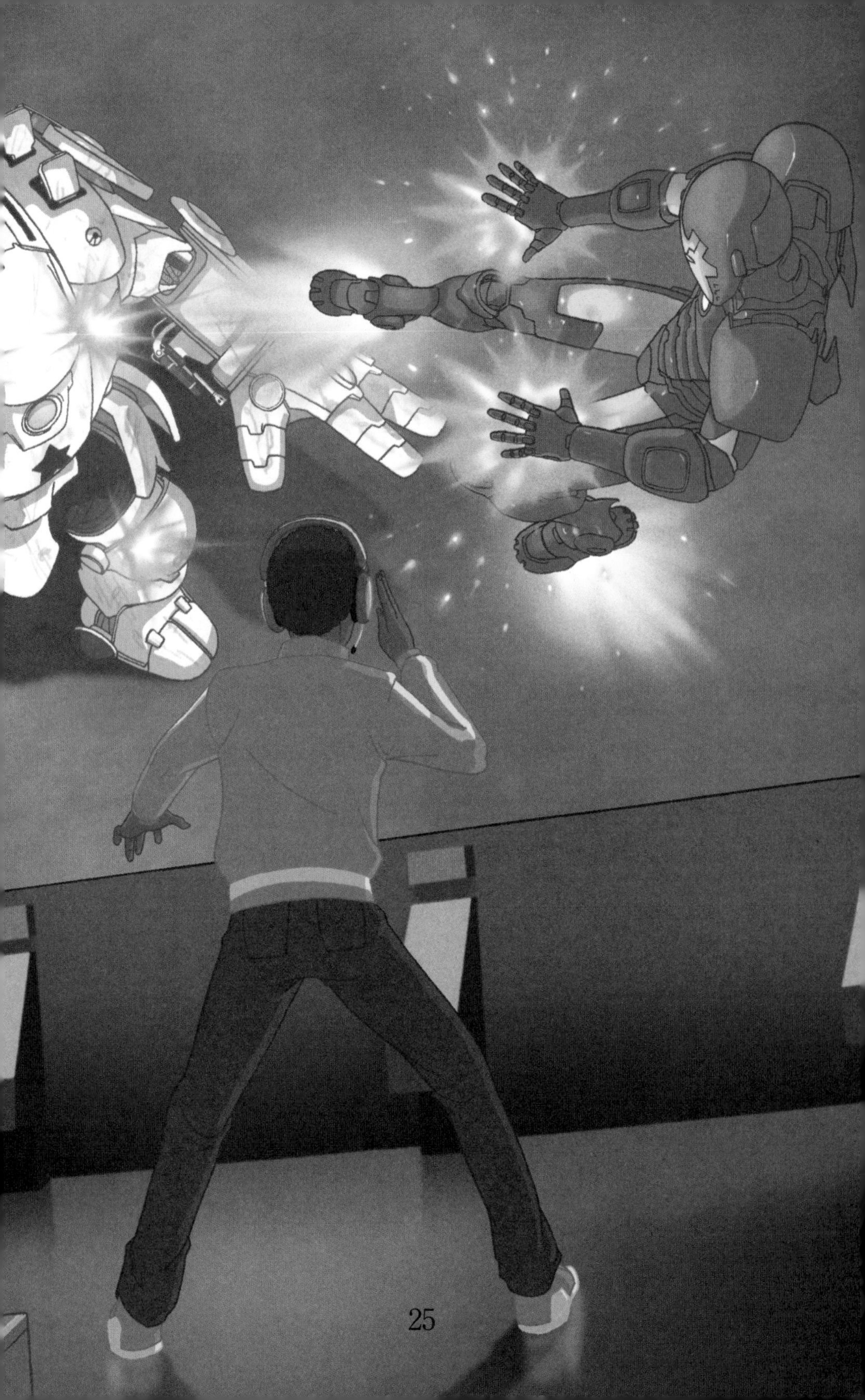

Without warning,
the Crimson Dynamo
set a gas truck on fire.

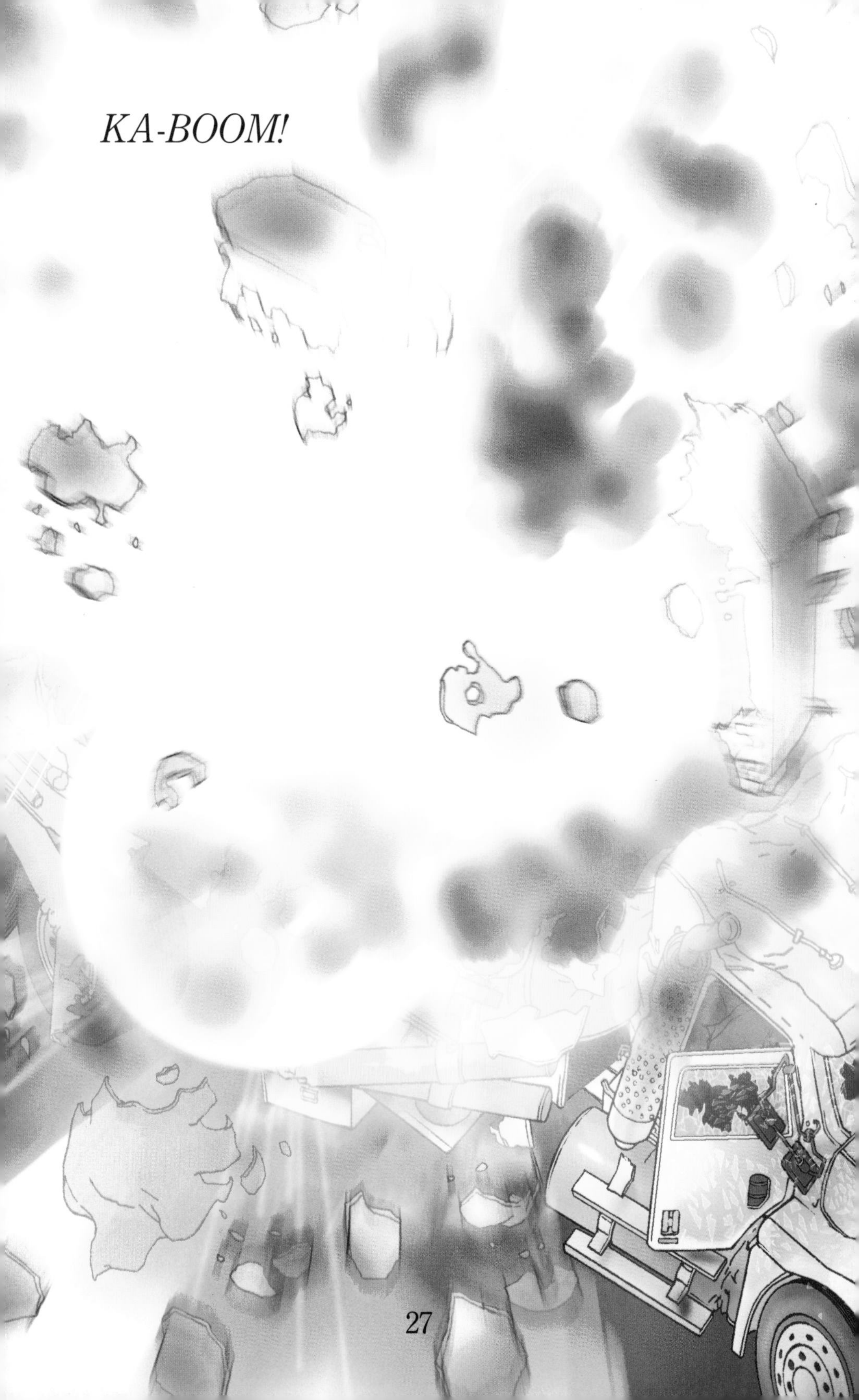
KA-BOOM!

Iron Man flew out of the fire.

He was not hurt.

Iron Man raced ahead
to Project Pegasus.

When Iron Man reached the lab,

he met a scientist

named Dr. Harkov.

Harkov told him that
the Crimson Dynamo
was a man named Ivan Vanko.

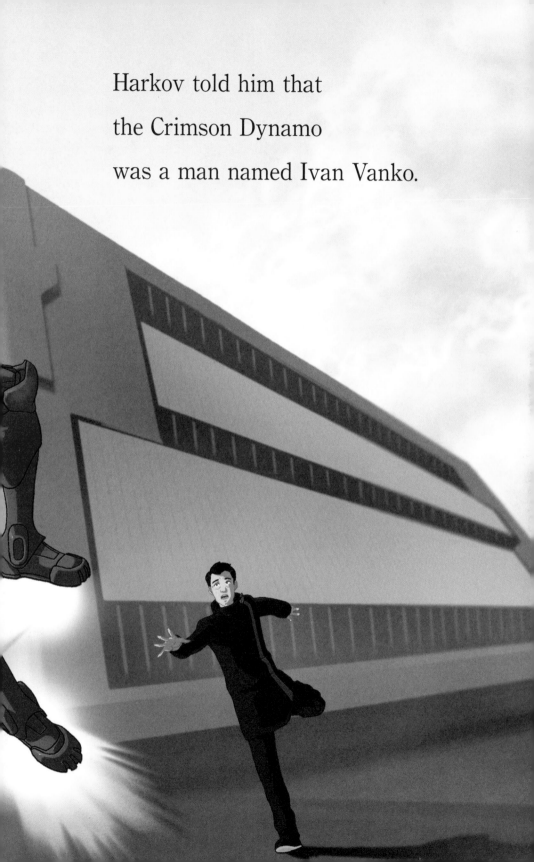

There had been

an accident

on a space mission.

Vanko had been

left in space!

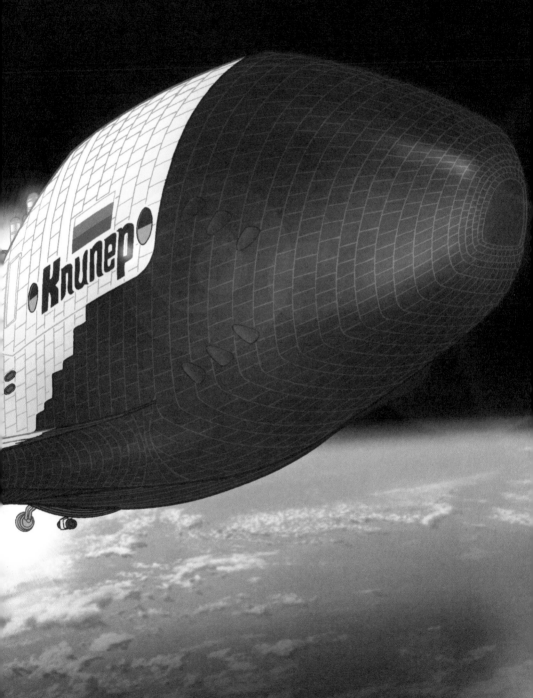

Iron Man was shocked!
He would never
leave his friends behind.

THOOM! THOOM! THOOM!

The Crimson Dynamo

smashed through the steel doors!

"Harkov!"

Vanko shouted.

"Where is my family?

I cannot find them!"

Tony told Pepper

to find Vanko's

family—fast!

Iron Man stepped
between Vanko
and Harkov.

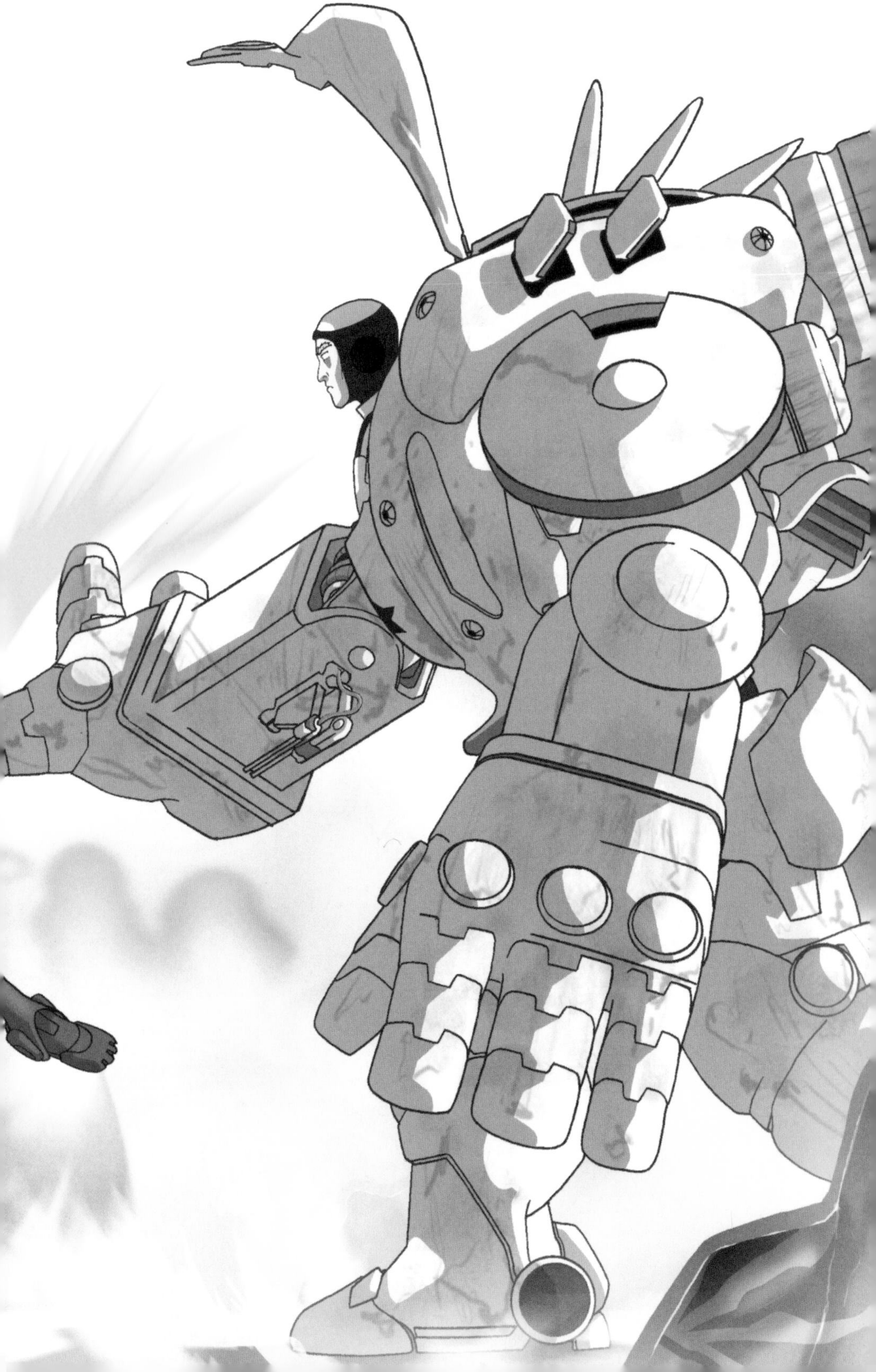

Iron Man had to
slow Vanko down.
He used his
repulsor rays
to create a cloud
of dirt and dust.

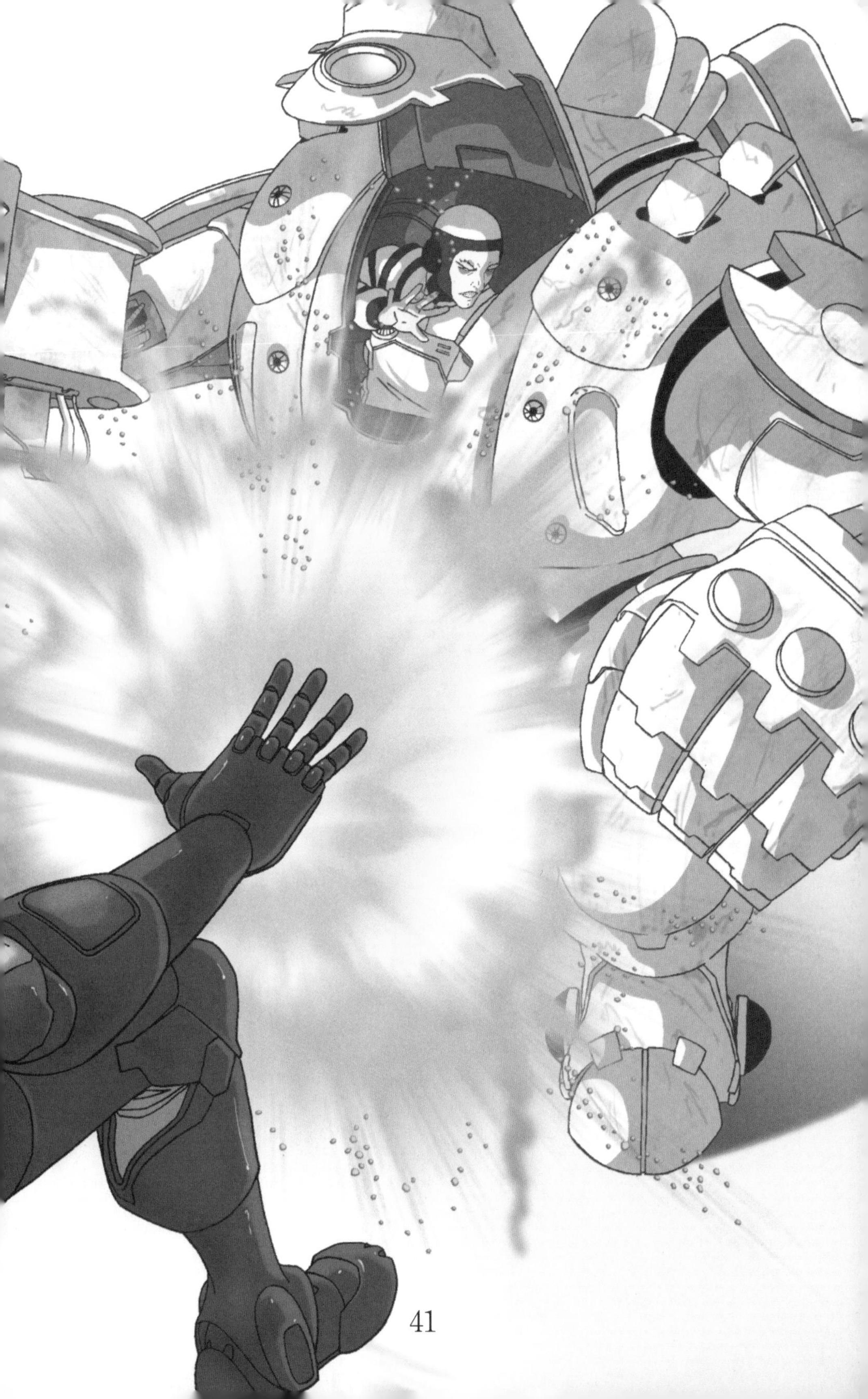

Vanko grabbed Iron Man.

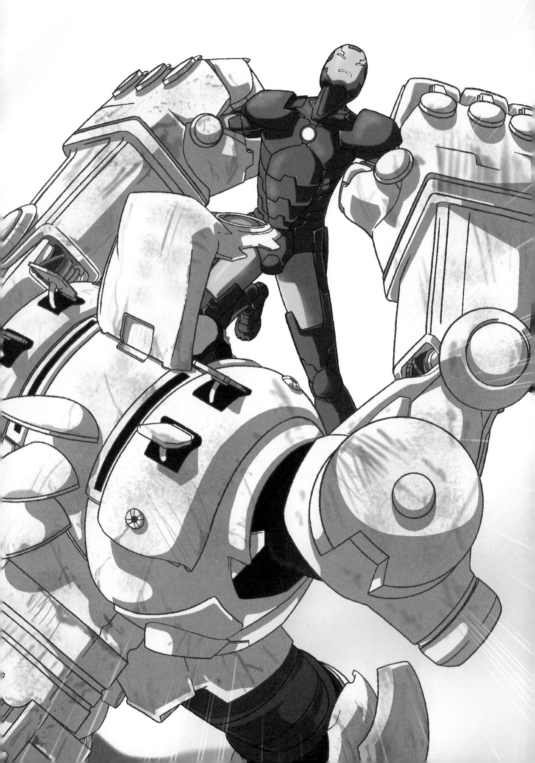

Just then,
a little boy
ran into the lab.
Pepper had found
Vanko's family.
"Daddy!" the boy cried.

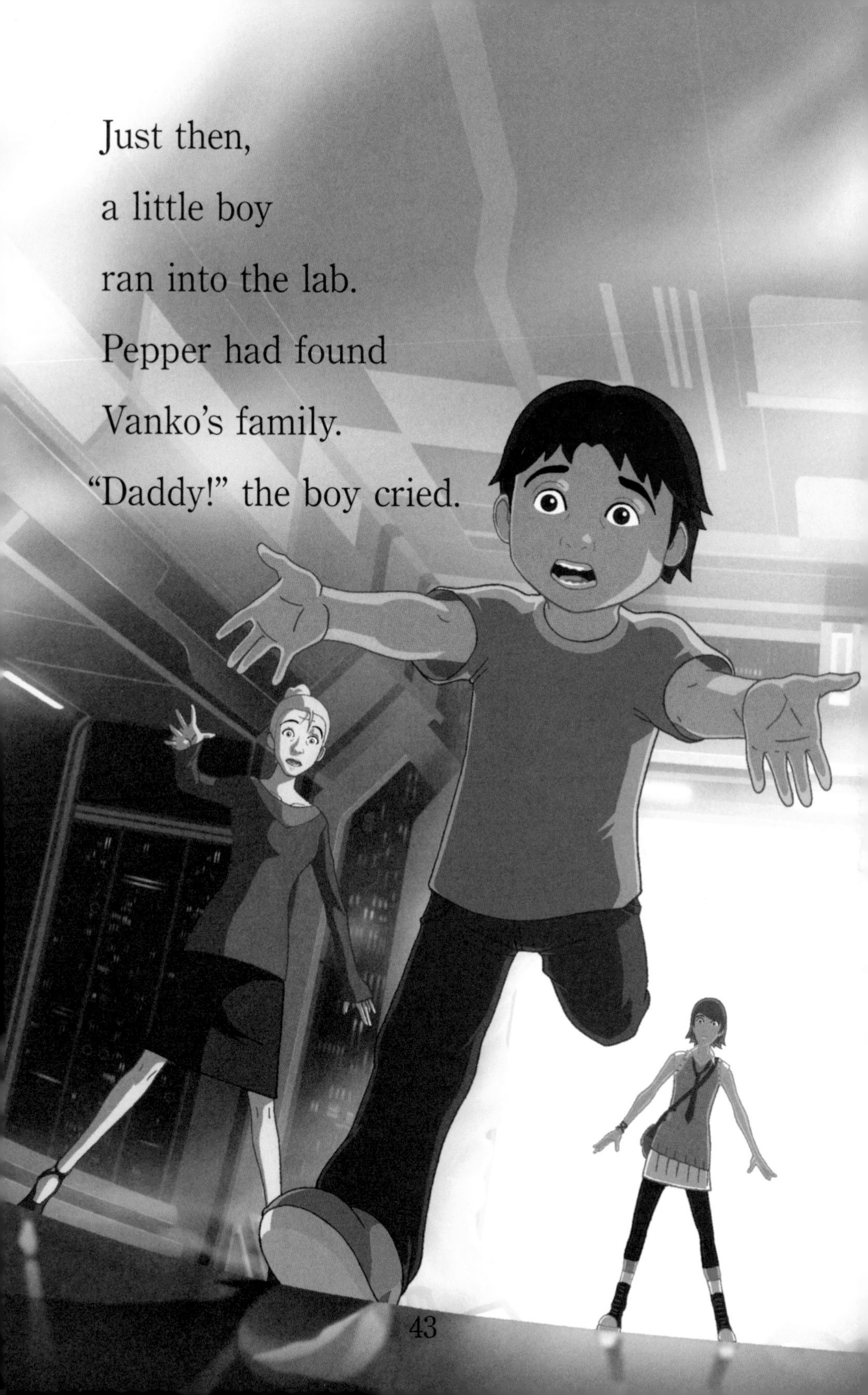

Vanko was so happy!
He took off his armor
and hugged his family.

The Crimson Dynamo
was no longer a threat.
Iron Man and his friends
had saved the day.

The next morning at school,
Rhodey and Pepper
were surprised.
Their science project
was a huge success!

"I would never
abandon my friends,"
Tony said.

Tony had
finished it
before class.